studio fun
INTERNATIONAL

Studio Fun International
An imprint of Printers Row Publishing Group
A division of Readerlink Distribution Services, LLC
10350 Barnes Canyon Road, Suite 100, San Diego, CA 92121
www.studiofun.com

ISBN: 978-0-7944-4378-8
Manufactured, printed, and assembled in Heshan, China.
First printing, January 2019. LP/01/19
23 22 21 20 19 1 2 3 4 5

VOLUME II

STAR WARS™

SEARCH AND FIND

The harsh desert planet of Jakku is littered with forgotten wreckage from the fallen Empire. A scavenger named Rey lives here in solitude, eking out a meager existence as the shadow of the First Order grows darker.

While Rey counts the days until her family returns, find these belongings that help her feel at home:

Stormtrooper FN-2187—Finn for short—needs help defecting from the First Order. So he springs Resistance Pilot Poe Dameron from Kylo Ren's clutches. Poe is happy to help—and to find his droid BB-8, who holds coordinates to Luke Skywalker's location.

As Poe and Finn (attempt to) commandeer a TIE fighter, help them steer clear of these obstacles:

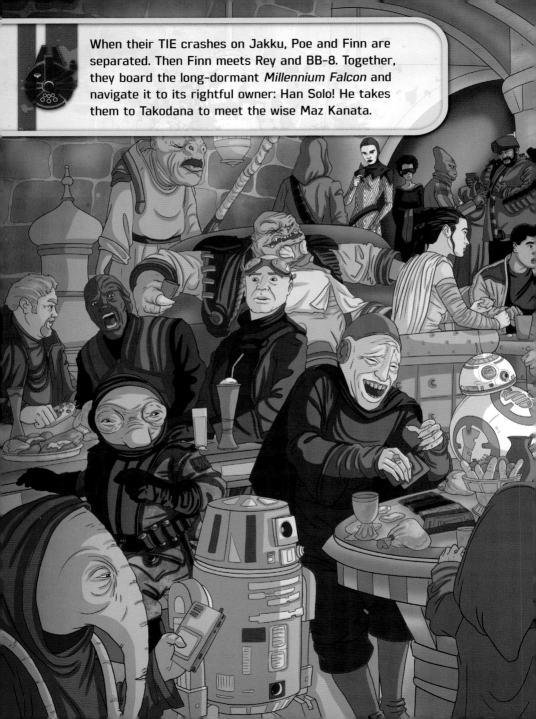

When their TIE crashes on Jakku, Poe and Finn are separated. Then Finn meets Rey and BB-8. Together, they board the long-dormant *Millennium Falcon* and navigate it to its rightful owner: Han Solo! He takes them to Takodana to meet the wise Maz Kanata.

While Maz looks closely at Finn, find this galactic bric-a-brac in her castle:

In Maz's castle, Rey discovers Luke Skywalker's lightsaber and has a Force vision. Frightened, she runs outside, leaving the relic behind. But instead of a breath of fresh air, she finds the First Order! Rey confronts Kylo Ren as her friends—and the Resistance—counterattack.

Fight for the light by spotting these by-products of battle:

When confronted with planet-sized weapons, Han knows: there's always a way to blow it up. So when the X-wings are having a tough time destroying Starkiller's thermal oscillator from the outside, Han and Chewie blow it up from the inside.

Watch out for Kylo Ren and these stormtroopers:

Kylo Ren overpowered Rey on Takodana, but he quickly realizes the Force is strong with her. Soon, she's using his power to learn the ways of the Force. Now, in the forest on the collapsing Starkiller Base, Rey is a force to be reckoned with.

Avoid these falling trees in this battle between light and dark:

Starkiller Base is vanquished, but Kylo Ren has escaped. Thanks to Rey and her friends, BB-8 brought Luke Skywalker's coordinates back to the Resistance. On their behalf, Rey travels to the planet Ahch-To, hoping to enlist Luke's help.

While Rey persuades the last Jedi to join the Resistance, look for these rocky features:

Meanwhile, Poe is busy doing some persuading of his own. He and BB-8 are making runs through the First Order's latest assault fleet to clear the way for the Resistance bomber squadron, headed by ace pilot Paige.

BB-8 will keep the coordinates straight. *You* look out for these First Order ships:

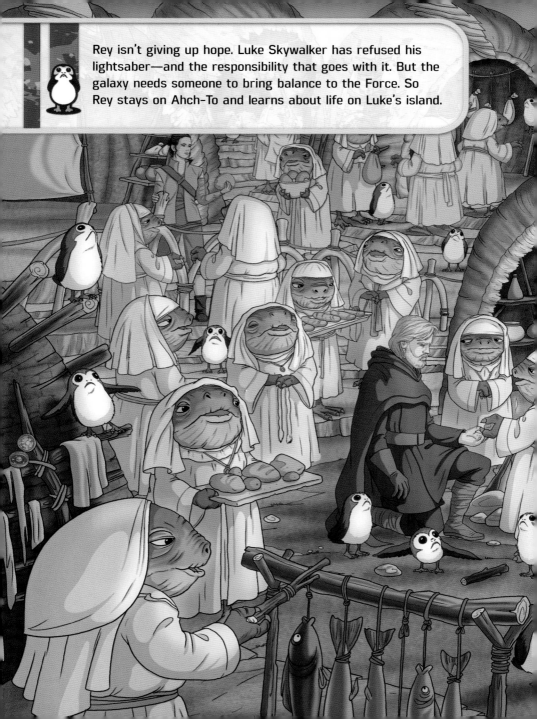

Rey isn't giving up hope. Luke Skywalker has refused his lightsaber—and the responsibility that goes with it. But the galaxy needs someone to bring balance to the Force. So Rey stays on Ahch-To and learns about life on Luke's island.

As the Caretakers prepare a meal, find Luke, their guests, and the things they never leave home without:

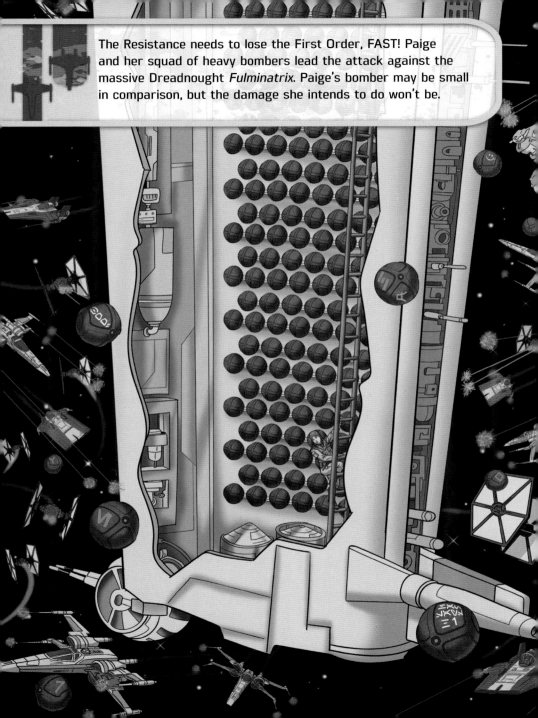

The Resistance needs to lose the First Order, FAST! Paige and her squad of heavy bombers lead the attack against the massive Dreadnought *Fulminatrix*. Paige's bomber may be small in comparison, but the damage she intends to do won't be.

Before Paige sends her *explosive* regards to the First Order, find these bombs:

Turn to the back of the book to translate these messages.

General Leia Organa discovers that the First Order's new technology can track her ship through hyperspace. But she and the Resistance maintain that spark of hope that keeps their cause alive. Kylo Ren and General Hux intend to snuff out that spark.

Help the Resistance keep ahead of these First Order ships:

Every time Chewie lets his guard down, the porgs flutter all over him. Onboard the *Millennium Falcon*, Ahch-To's mischievous avian creatures have gotten themselves into plenty of trouble . . . and circuitry!

Help Chewie round up these porgs before their feathers clog the alluvial dampers:

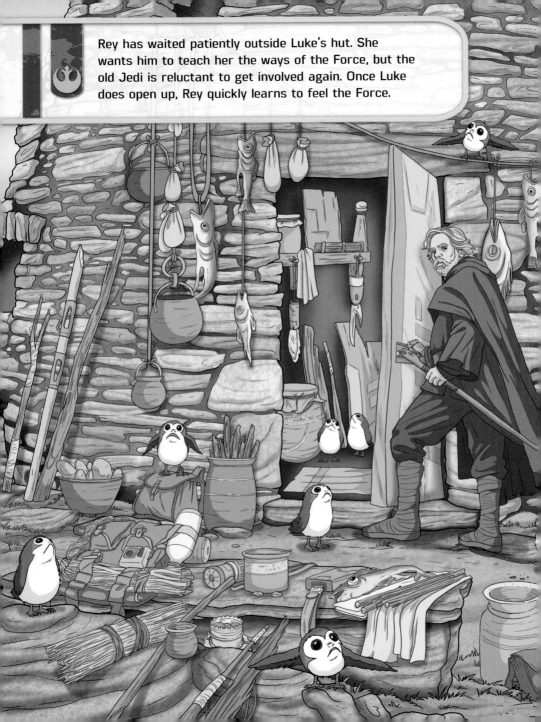

Rey has waited patiently outside Luke's hut. She wants him to teach her the ways of the Force, but the old Jedi is reluctant to get involved again. Once Luke does open up, Rey quickly learns to feel the Force.

Reach out and find these things that belong to the Jedi Master:

The Canto Bight casino is a glitzy, glamorous game room filled with some of the galaxy's wealthiest—and a Master Codebreaker. Finn and Rose try not to stick out, but it doesn't take a Canto Cop to spot them.

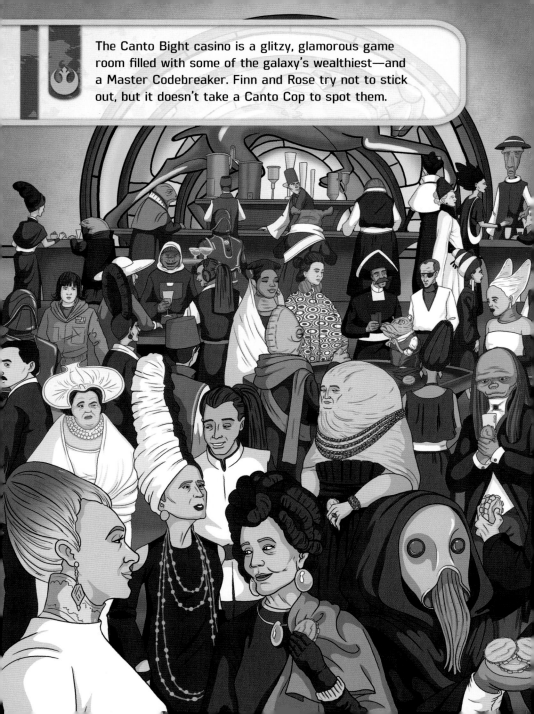

Look for the man with the red plom bloom on his lapel and these other casino patrons:

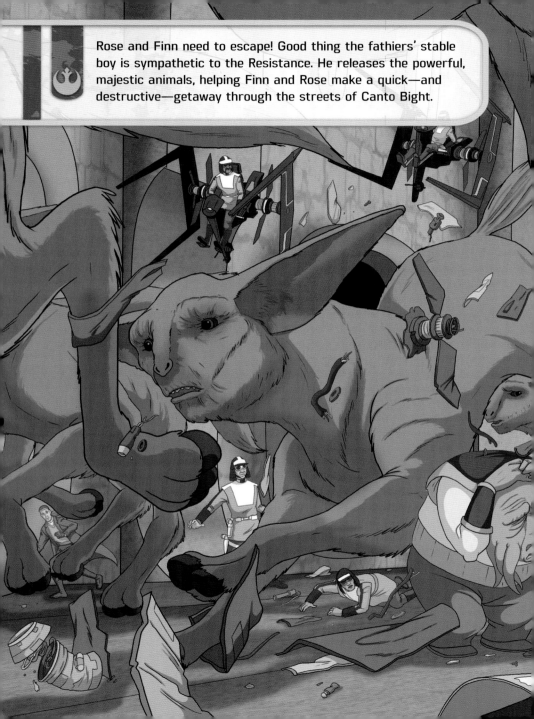

Rose and Finn need to escape! Good thing the fathiers' stable boy is sympathetic to the Resistance. He releases the powerful, majestic animals, helping Finn and Rose make a quick—and destructive—getaway through the streets of Canto Bight.

Find these officers and steer them away from the fathier stampede:

Red crystals erupt through the ground of planet Crait as the Resistance faces off against the First Order. They are outnumbered, have outdated technology, and are running out of time before their base's blast doors give out. But that doesn't mean they're giving up!

Find these ski speeders operated by Rose, Finn, Poe, and other members of the Resistance:

Hurry back to Rey's home and look for this
scavenged stuff she could trade for food rations:

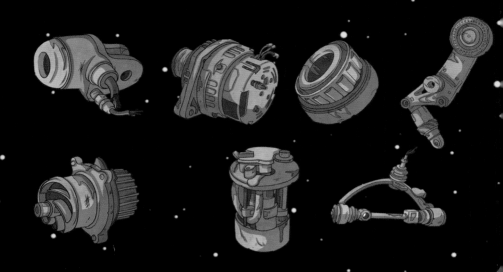

Hitch a ride to Maz's ancient watering hole and remember
not to stare at these smugglers, aliens, and other patrons:

Board the *Finalizer* and find these untethered TIE fighters:

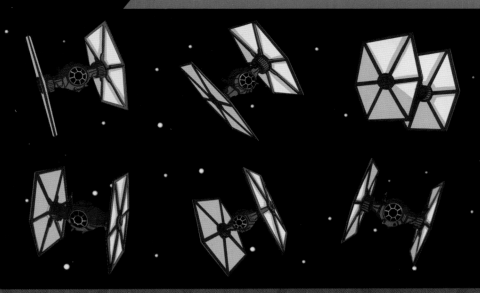

Trek back to Takodana and watch out for these stormtroopers on the offensive:

Sneak around Starkiller's precinct 47 and help Han and Chewie plant 20 explosives.

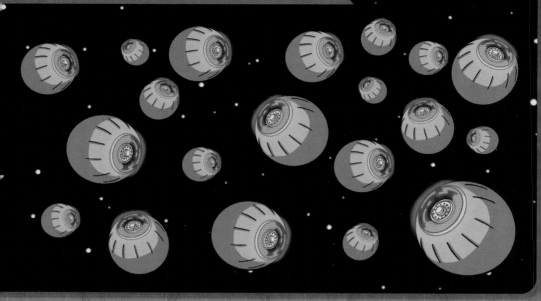

Fly back to Starkiller's forest and find these heroic X-wings overhead:

Visit Ahch-To and observe these native island dwellers:

Fire up your converters to rendezvous with the bomber squadron and these Resistance ships:

Travel back to Ahch-To and meet these
Caretakers who maintain the ancient Jedi site:

Defeat the First Order! Blast back to Paige's bomber
and find the Aurebesh letters that spell RESISTANCE:

Aurebesh Key

A	B	C	D	E	F	G	H	I	J	K	L	M

N	O	P	Q	R	S	T	U	V	W	X	Y	Z

The *Millennium Falcon* isn't just a bucket of bolts—it's also a hunk of junk stuffed with memories. Hit the hyperdrive and find these relics from past adventures. Punch it!

Jump to the battle in space and find these Resistance ships:

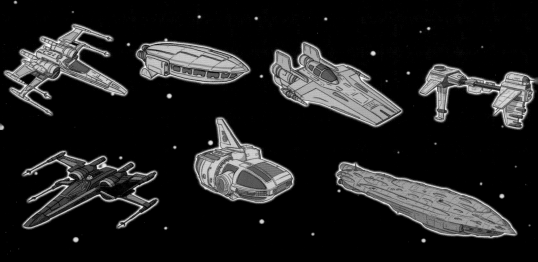

Luke's diet on Ahch-To consists mainly of fish. Having lived in the Jakku desert nearly all her life, Rey is interested in the island's aquatic creatures. Help her find some tasty ones back at Luke's hut:

Roll the dice back at the casino, and see how many tokens you can find:

x20

The Resistance never misses a chance to chip away at the First Order. Cruise back to Crait and spot these bits of damage to the TIE fighters and walkers: